Mary De
Room 2

The Eggs Are Hatching!

Story by Monica and Antonio Incisa

Illustrations by **Monica Incisa**

 Greenwillow Books, New York

To Veronica and Daniele

Pen and ink, colored pencils, and watercolor paints were used for the full-color art. The text type is ITC Caslon No. 224.

Text copyright © 1988 by Monica and Antonio Incisa
Illustrations copyright © 1988 by Monica Incisa
Greenwillow Books, a division of William Morrow & Company, Inc., 105 Madison Avenue, New York, N.Y. 10016.
Printed in Singapore by Tien Wah Press
First Edition   10 9 8 7 6 5 4 3 2 1

Library of Congress Cataloging-in-Publication Data
Incisa, Monica.   The eggs are hatching!
Summary: While waiting for their mother's new eggs to hatch, the plover chicks go along the riverbank to visit the crocodile and help her in her vigil over her own eggs.
[1. Plovers—Fiction.   2. Crocodiles—Fiction.
3. Eggs—Fiction]   I. Incisa, Antonio.   II. Title.
PZ7.I36Eg   1988   [E]   86-27100
ISBN 0-688-06986-X   ISBN 0-688-06987-8 (lib. bdg.)

One very hot day in the spring three young plovers were helping their mother keep her eggs cool. They brought damp sand to cover them. They wet their wings in the river and flapped them over the nest. They were so excited, they splashed each other and jumped about.

"Be careful," scolded their mother. "I think you
   have helped enough."
"Let's go visit the crocodile," said one of the chicks.
"She's waiting for her eggs to hatch, too."

On the way they met a lion and her cubs.
"Guess what, we will soon have brothers and
sisters," they told the lion.

"Hello," they said to the hippopotamus. "How is the baby?
Mother says our eggs will soon be hatching."

"Hello, hello," the plovers called
as they flew by their friends.

The crocodile was glad to see them.
"What a lot of eggs you have," said the plover
   chicks. "Our mother only has three."
"Easier to keep three cool in this heat than
   all of these," said the crocodile.
"We can help you," said the plovers.
"That would be nice," said the crocodile.
"Then I can rest a bit."

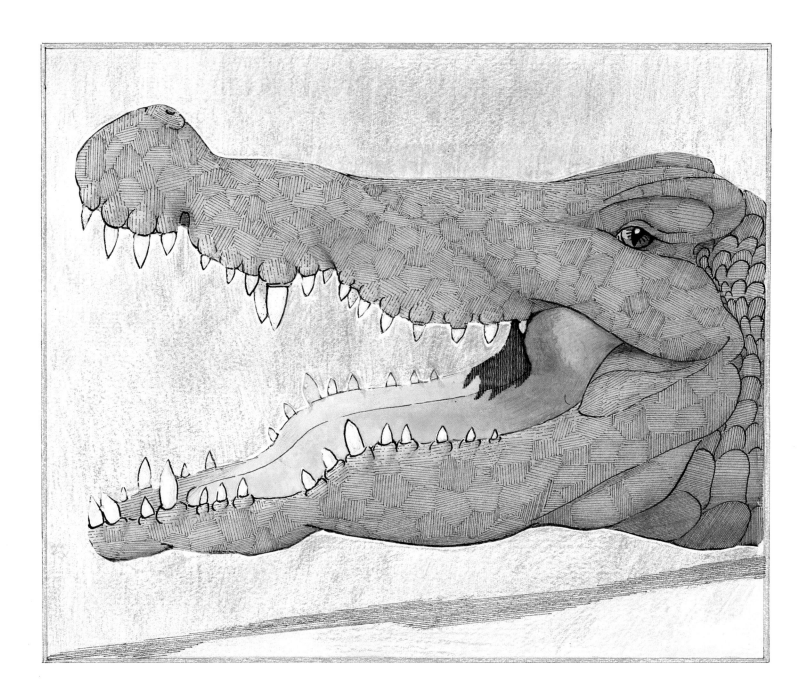

The chicks ran into the water and out. They flapped their wings and shook their feathers over the crocodile's eggs. Back and forth, back and forth they went.

The crocodile lay under a nearby tree. "That's enough for now," she said after a while. "Come and sit by me."

The chicks flew over to the crocodile.
The crocodile watched her eggs.
Suddenly there was a crack.
One egg began to hatch,
then another and another.

The crocodile and the chicks rushed over and
began brushing the sand away from the eggs.
As the last baby crocodile broke out of its shell,
the chicks looked at one another.

"Aren't they big," the chicks said. "Maybe
our mother's eggs are hatching, too.
Let's go home and see."
"Wait," said the crocodile. "I'll go with you.
I must take my babies to the water so they
can have their first swim."

"I've brought your chicks back," said the crocodile to the plover. "They were a big help with my eggs."
"I'm so glad," said the plover. "What handsome babies you have, and they are swimming already."
"Yes," said the crocodile proudly.

The plover chicks had gone straight to
the nest. Suddenly there was a crack, and
another and another. The plover and
the crocodile hurried over.

"See," said the plover chicks.
"We knew just when to come home."